I Miss My Daddy

Jill Pike

Illustrated by Cady Driver

ISBN: 978-1-4834-5757-4 (sc)
ISBN: 978-1-4834-5756-7 (hc)
ISBN: 978-1-4834-5758-1 (e)

Library of Congress Control Number: 2016914725

Lulu Publishing Services rev. date: 10/31/2016

Dedicated with love to my sons
Joshua, Joseph, and Zachary

I miss the way my daddy tickled me right before bedtime. Mama acted mad and said, "Settle down!," but sometimes I caught her smiling.

I miss building sand castles together at the beach, letting the wet, gritty sand drip from our fingertips to make tall towers.

I miss snuggling in my daddy's lap while he sat in his big chair watching TV. His faded jeans were soft and worn. With his arms around me, I knew nothing scary would ever happen to me.

I sleep in one of my daddy's old T-shirts. It looks like a dress on me, but I don't care. When his big shirt wraps around me, I imagine he is hugging me.

A new kid moved into the house across the street. His dad is the baseball coach and math teacher at the high school. I see them playing catch together in their front yard, and I remember when my dad and I did that. The new kid asked me where my dad was. I lied and said he was a reporter and had to travel a lot because of his job.

A few days later, I shoved Tommy and knocked him down when he stepped on my foot, even though deep down I knew he didn't mean to. I threw my lunch money on the floor and said a bad word when the teacher sent me to the back of the line for talking on the way to the cafeteria. Then I got sent to the principal, who called Mama to come to my school for a conference.

I sure wish the principal had sent me home for a day or two, because the next day we were supposed to make Father's Day cards. The kids at my table drew pictures of themselves doing fun things with their dads. I broke all my crayons and then pretended to be sick so I could lie down on the cot in the nurse's office.

Most days after school, I talk to my dog, Rusty, about how I wish my daddy was back home with us. He looks at me with his sad, brown beagle eyes and licks the tears on my face with his warm, rough tongue. I rub the soft, black fur on his back and feel his heart beating next to mine as he lies across my chest.

During the day, Mama acts happy and smiles a lot. At night in her bedroom, she turns her radio up loud, but I can still hear her crying.

Last Saturday, Mama and I bought ice cream cones and drove to the park. She sat across from me at a picnic table and looked at me. Then Mama said, "It's normal to feel sad and angry that Daddy is not here, but he would not want us to stay that way forever." I know she is right, but I don't know how to stop feeling this way. I just wish things could be the way they used to be.

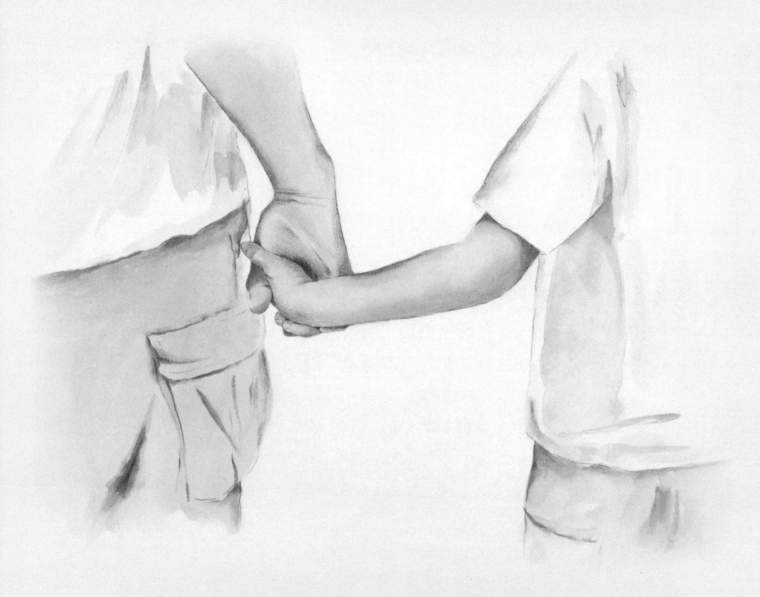

I worry that I will not always remember the sound of his quiet voice and his funny, high-pitched laugh or the feel of his big hand wrapped around mine. What if I forget the clean, minty way he smelled when he put on his aftershave?

One day Mama got an idea. She said, "Today we are going to make a memory book about Daddy." We glued photographs on the blank pages. There was a photo of Daddy and me on a Tilt-A-Whirl at the state fair, laughing as the ride slung us around. Another photo was one taken on our family's trip to the zoo last summer. We were standing in front of a fence with three giraffes in the background.

On some of the pages in the book, Mama and I wrote down things we remembered about Daddy, like our "tickle times" and how he loved to bake his special, extra-chocolatey brownies on the weekends.

Mama and I worked all morning, and by lunchtime we had finished twenty pages. Looking at the memory book makes me feel better. My daddy and I really had a lot of fun times together. Now I don't have to worry about forgetting things we did, since they are right there in the book.

The photograph on the last page is my favorite. The two of us are holding a big bunch of red, yellow, blue, and green balloons we bought to decorate for my birthday a few months ago. We joked about floating away as we held on to all those balloons.

After my party, we let them go one by one and watched them as they drifted up to my grandma and grandpa in heaven and to friends and relatives who lived too far to come to my party.

Now, every time I go to the grocery store with Mama, I get a balloon. When I get home, I go outside and let my balloon go to send it to my daddy as a gift. Sometimes I write a short message on it.

Mama says that our love and memories keep us connected to Daddy. She says, "Daddy still loves us even if he isn't here with us anymore, because love never ends."

A few days ago, I talked with the school counselor, Mrs. Jacobs. She told me that there are a lot of kids who don't have dads living at home with them. Some dads are far away in the military, and some are very sick in a hospital. Some dads are in prison, some live in other states because of divorces or jobs, and others have died. It made me feel a little better to realize that I am not the only one missing a father.

While I was in her office, Mrs. Jacobs called my mom and invited us to a cookout with a group of families. They meet every month and do fun things together, like picnics, ballgames, and field trips. These families are like us—a mom and kids with no dad at home. Mama and I went to the cookout, and it wasn't so bad. The moms sat at picnic tables and talked while the kids played ball.

When my kickball team was in the field, I tried to catch a fly ball. I missed, and the rubber ball bounced right off the top of my head. It didn't hurt, but I was embarrassed. All the kids laughed. At first, I got mad and felt my face turning red. Then, suddenly, I could hear my daddy's words in my heart telling me to just laugh along with them. So I did, and it felt good. Nobody was really trying to be mean to me. I guess I must have looked kind of funny.

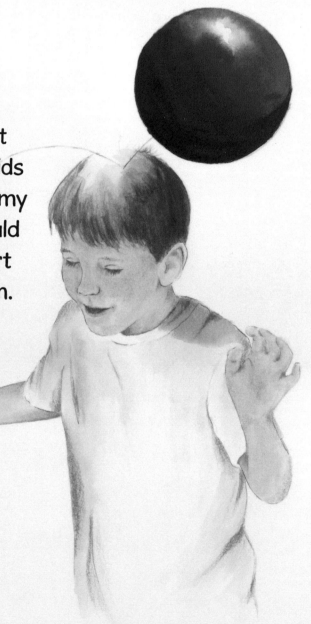

Ever since that picnic when I heard Daddy's voice in my heart, I try to be better in school because I know it is what he would want me to do. The next time my class makes Father's Day cards, I'm going to make one, too. I'll take it home, tie it to a balloon, send it to my daddy, and imagine his smiling face as he reads it.

CPSIA information can be obtained at www.ICGtesting.com
Printed in the USA
LVIW01n2252130817
544896LV00003B/8